Selected for First Partner Jennifer Siebel Newsom's 2021 Summer Book Club.

This book is provided by the Summer @ Your Library project, which is supported by the U.S. Institute of Museum and Library Services under the provisions of the Library Services and Technology Act, administered in California by the State Librarian.

My First Day

My First Day

written and illustrated by
Phùng Nguyên Quang
&
Huỳnh Kim Liên

MAKE ME A WORLD

New York

Where the great river, mother Mekong,
tumbles into the endless sea . . . that is where I live.

I wake up with the sun creeping into the sky
and wait for tide and time to bring to me my
little open boat.
Today is the first day.

This is the first time I've made
this trip on my own, weaving
through floodwaters and forests.
Mama said I'm big enough now
to go by myself. Papa said to be
careful because that's what
papas do.

I paddle out into the floodwaters,
past yesterdays and all the things
I didn't know.

I set out upon the waves and begin my adventure.

The river swells—water stretches
as far as forever in front of me.
There is still a world to learn.

As the skies grow dark with rain, the rough waters bring me to the opening of the mangrove forest.

It's different when you're alone
in the unfamiliar hallways of the
forest.

I hear the chatter of a classroom
full of animals as I move by.

The mangroves hide a
thousand eyes, all looking
at me.

When you don't know
a place, it can be scary.

The jungle calls your name, asks you
to be brave.
  Still, fear slithers in like a python.

But what you know can
make a difference, turn
the unfamiliar into family.
 I get to trace the edges of
my path—do it for
myself, write my name
across the blackboard
of the river.

The sky is a crayon box full of colors for me to take flight— grow my own wings—a dance of storks and new worlds.

Schools of fish glint
beneath the waves.

Even water buffalo, galumphing near the shore (finally, the shore!), bellow their welcome.

Hello, buffalo!

Hello, friends!

Hello, first day of school—my journey ends.

- The Mekong River area has one of the world's most diverse collections of flora and fauna. Many amazing creatures live in the Mekong River, some of which are found nowhere else. These include the giant freshwater stingray, the Mekong giant catfish, and Irrawaddy dolphins.
- Today we need to protect the river from overuse, which puts the resources of the river area at risk.

MAKE ME A WORLD

Dear Reader,

There is a kind of puzzle that I remember from childhood, often on the backs of cereal boxes or on the placemat at restaurants—"find the difference between these two pictures." A lot of childhood games rely on finding which "one of these things is not like the other," as the song says.

As important as difference is, and the recognition of difference, the world isn't made up of neatly defined categories, of "sames" and "differents." Especially as the world grows smaller, as technology, immigration, and ease of travel bring our living rooms, dinner plates, and media landscapes closer, almost overlapping, the idea of same and different has fundamentally shifted. Things are more often some combination of same and different. Strangeness and familiarity are braided together.

This braiding of sames and differents often yields great results. I think about the ways that music travels, how songs move from one culture to another, changing lyrics and languages, but, at the center, holding some of the original intention. The way that Italian spaghetti is Asian, or English tea is from India, or American tap dance is Irish and African.

My First Day is a book about something familiar to most of us, but also it is different. The book collapses the space between same and different and in doing so creates something very close to wonder in our everyday. For Phùng Nguyên Quang and Huỳnh Kim Liên, an author-illustrator team as widely imaginative as spaghetti or tap dance, it is precisely the chance to depict this familiarity in all its strangeness that allows them to rediscover the magic of first journeys, the magic of first steps on your own, the magic that is *My First Day.*

Christopher Myers

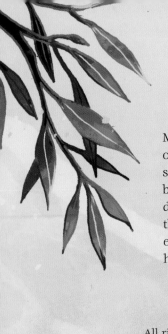

To all the kids who yearn to learn out there

MAKE ME A WORLD is an imprint dedicated to exploring the vast possibilities of contemporary childhood. We strive to imagine a universe in which no young person is invisible, in which no kid's story is erased, in which no glass ceiling presses down on the dreams of a child. Then we publish books for that world, where kids ask hard questions and we struggle with them together, where dreams stretch from eons ago into the future and we do our best to provide road maps to where these young folks want to be. We make books where the children of today can see themselves and each other. When presented with fences, with borders, with limits, with all the kinds of chains that hobble imaginations and hearts, we proudly say—no.

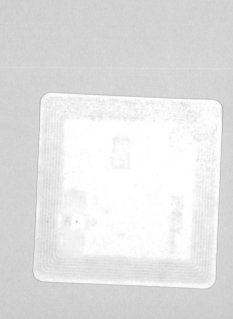